PIRATE M◯use

For Jack and Grace.
My world. My inspiration.

First published 2020 by Telltale Tots Publishing

ISBN: 978-1-9162549-0-9

Text and illustrations copyright © Kirstie Watson 2020

PIRATE MOUSE

Kirstie Watson

Sirma Karaguiozova

In a dark, dusty corner of an old ship
lived a mouse; a pirate mouse.

She was brave. "Arrrrgh!"

She was rough and tough. "Grrrrr!"

And she loved nothing more than a good old
treasure hunt.

"Ye touch me loot, ye feel me boot!"

But Pirate Mouse was all alone, long since abandoned
by her shipmates.

Something about 'the mess' they'd said, as
they hurried off in the lifeboats.

It was true, she wasn't the tidiest of pirates. Her cabin was far from shipshape, and she hadn't washed in years.

Water was just not her thing.

But still, she couldn't understand their problem.

One day, Pirate Mouse set off on an exciting treasure hunt, and it wasn't long before something interesting caught her eye.

"Shiver me timbers! It must be treasure!" she said.

But she couldn't quite see what it was, because something was in the way. It was...

SPLASH!

... an enormous soggy MOP. It swept carelessly across her path, splashing water everywhere it went.

"Arrrrr!" she yelled, as she scurried away.

Her hunt was not over yet, though.
Once the coast was clear,
she set off again.

But, little did she know, another obstacle
lurked around the corner...

SPLOSH!

A gigantic bucket appeared, spilling water everywhere.

"Arrrr! Scallywag!" she said crossly.

Once she was sure the bucket had gone, she set off again to claim her prize.

But, while she'd been keeping an eye out for the bucket, she hadn't noticed the clouds gathering in the sky...

Drip drop drip drop!

It started to rain. "Arrrrr! Son of a seadog!" she huffed.

Later, with a break in the weather, Pirate Mouse decided to give it another go.

But she couldn't have imagined...

CRASH! FLASH!

...the storm that suddenly swept in.

Thunder clapped and lightning forked, as huge ocean waves crashed over the sides of the great ship.

"Batten down the hatches!" she shouted, as she hurried for shelter.

But there was no escaping it this time. She was absolutely...

SOAKING WET!

As she drip-dried and waited out the storm, she realised
two things:

One, water wasn't so bad. In fact, she now felt a little...
clean.

And two, she simply MUST complete her treasure hunt.
Otherwise, it would all be for nothing.

So, off she went. More determined than ever.

But there, blocking her path was an awful, ghastly, monstrous... PUDDLE!

This time, though, she would not let a little water defeat her.

So, she put on her wellies. Then...

...she darted and dashed...

...zigzagged and weaved...

...jumped and danced...

...right around the puddle.

And this time...

...she made it.

"Yo ho ho!" she cheered.

"But wait, what be this... treasure?"

There, amongst the booty, was something quite unexpected.

It was feathery... It was sobbing and sniffing... It was...

A puffin; a pirate puffin!

"Hello," sniffed the puffin. "Can you help me? I'm stuck in this net. I was just looking for somewhere safe to hide my treasure. But every time I find a place to keep it, I forget where it is. And now I'm stuck and all alone! Waaaaaaa," he wailed.

Even though she was a rough, tough pirate, she couldn't help feeling sad for the puffin. Pirate Mouse knew only too well what it was like to be all alone.

"Don't ye worry," she said, "I'll soon set ye free!"

So she darted and dashed, zigzagged and weaved, jumped and danced and, with a swish of her cutlass, the puffin was freed.

"Oh thank you, THANK YOU!" said the puffin. "How can I ever repay you?" he asked.

Pirate Mouse thought for a moment.

"Ye like hunting for treasure?"

"Oh yes, very much," said the puffin. "And I find all kinds of treasure under the sea."

"It's simple really. I dive down, find things and stash them somewhere safe. But I always forget where. Then again, the fun's in finding the treasure, don't you agree?"

"Hmmm. No..." said Pirate Mouse thoughtfully,
"...but ye've given me an idea."

"When ye find some treasure, bring it 'ere and I'll keep it safe in me dark, dusty corner. Then ye'll always know where t' find it and, best of all, I won't EVER need t' get wet!"

And so, Pirate Mouse and Pirate Puffin became the finest treasure hunting pirate crew on the Seven Seas.

But of course, they'd already found the greatest treasure of all.

The End.